TWO STORIES

TWO STORIES

VIRGINIA WOOLF

AND

MARK HADDON

HOGARTH PRESS

LONDON

1 3 5 7 9 10 8 6 4 2

Hogarth, an imprint of Vintage,
20 Vauxhall Bridge Road,
London SW1V 2SA

Hogarth is part of the Penguin Random House group of companies whose
addresses can be found at global.penguinrandomhouse.com.

'The Mark on the Wall' by Virginia Woolf first appeared
in *Two Stories*, published by the Hogarth Press in 1917

'St Brides Bay' and portrait of Virginia Woolf copyright © Mark Haddon 2017

Introductory material © Hogarth 2017

Mark Haddon has asserted his right to be identified as the author of this Work in
accordance with the Copyright, Designs and Patents Act 1988

First published by Hogarth in 2017

penguin.co.uk/vintage

A CIP catalogue record for this book is available from the British Library

ISBN 9781781090671

Printed and bound by Clays Ltd, St Ives plc

Penguin Random House is committed to a sustainable future for our business,
our readers and our planet. This book is made from Forest Stewardship Council®
certified paper.

CONTENTS

FROM HOGARTH HOUSE:
the making of *Two Stories*

Printing fever arrived at Hogarth House, Paradise Road, Richmond, in Spring 1917. 'We get so absorbed we can't stop; I see that real printing will devour one's entire life,' Virginia Woolf wrote to her sister in April 1917. Her husband, Leonard, wished they had never bought the 'cursed' hand-press as there was a serious risk he might 'never do anything else'. The dining room was requisitioned for the machine. The couple were consumed and delighted by their new interest. Their hands were permanently stained with ink.

'Nowhere else could we have started the Hogarth Press,' Virginia wrote as they left Richmond for Bloomsbury in 1924, 'whose very awkward beginning had risen in this very room, on this very green carpet. Here that strange offspring grew & throve; it ousted us from the dining room [...] & crept all over the house'. By then, with forty books published – twenty hand-printed by the Woolfs themselves, including *Prelude* by Katherine Mansfield and *Poems* by T.S. Eliot – the 'strange offspring' stood on sturdy legs. The Press went on to thrive during the 1930s, and although stricken by Virginia's death in 1941, Leonard and the Press would find safe harbour at the established publishers Chatto & Windus shortly after the war, where it continues to this day.

The early titles, often handmade, were seldom beautiful. As Leonard later put it, the Woolfs weren't interested in making finely produced books 'which are not meant to be read'; plain printing and simple design were sufficient. In the 1920s and 30s, cover art by Vanessa Bell and others created a new mood, but in 1917 the urgent thing was to master the craft, and decide what to print.

There was much shared curiosity in acquiring a press. The Woolfs had moved into Hogarth House in 1915, and their early time there had been dominated by Virginia's recovery from mental breakdown. Leonard was exempt from military call-up owing to hand tremors, and his wife's illness. But as her health improved, the house became a place of possibility. And Leonard too was seeking diversion from the pressures of his work for the Fabian Society and the *New Statesman*.

Virginia had been taught book-binding in her teens. In 1916 she and Leonard had attempted to sign up for classes at St Bride's School of Printing, but discovered these were for unionised apprentices and not middle-class dilettantes. But they struck lucky in March the following year, as Leonard recalled:

> We were walking one afternoon up Farringdon Street from Fleet Street to Holborn Viaduct when we passed the Excelsior Printing Supply Co. […] Nearly all the implements of printing are materially attractive and we stared through the window at them rather like two hungry children gazing at buns and cakes in a baker shop window.

A century on, the building that housed Excelsior is

a down-at-heel Tandoori restaurant. Then, 'a very sympathetic man in a brown overall [...] extremely encouraging' listened to the Woolfs' dilemma. Perhaps he saw them coming: for £19 5s 5d he sold them 'a printing machine, type, chases, cases, and all the necessary implements' including 'a sixteen page pamphlet which would infallibly teach us how to print.'

On delivery, the machine turned out to have been broken in transit, and the Woolfs had to wait for a spare part. No matter, Virginia explained to her sister: 'the arrangement of the type is such a business that we shant be ready to start printing directly.' They were scouting for material from young poets and novelists but it wasn't yet clear what exactly they would be printing. Anyway, the Caslon Foundry type had arrived in 'great blocks' and Virginia's first task was to divide this into 'separate letters, and founts, and then put into the right partitions. The work of ages, especially when you mix the h's with the ns, as I did yesterday.'

The machine having been fixed, Leonard's job was to operate it. It sat on the dining-room table, 'an ordinary platen design; you worked it by pulling down the handle which brought the platen and paper up against the type in its chase.' Virginia's typesetting was an intricate and all-consuming job: using a composing stick to arrange and order each letter (in reverse and upside down), then adding spacing blocks between words and lines, all to exact measurements. Once a full page was ready, it was 'locked up' in the metal frame of the 'chase'; Leonard would ink the rollers and machine 'a fairly legible page'.

Then the solution became clear. They would each write a story, print the pair as a paper-covered

HOGARTH HOUSE
RICHMOND.

THE HOGARTH PRESS.

It is proposed to issue shortly a pamphlet containing two short stories by Leonard Woolf and Virginia Woolf,(price,includ--ing postage 1/2).

If you desire a copy to be sent to you,please fill up the form below and send it with a P. O. to L. S. Woolf at the above address before June   .

A limited edition only will be issued.

Please send   copy of Publication No. 1 to

for which 1 enclose P. O. for

NAME

ADDRESS

pamphlet and sell by subscription to their circle of friends. As if writing and printing weren't enough, the Woolfs now had to get down to the business of selling. Their first published work was in fact an advertisement, which Virginia sent to Lady Ottoline Morrell in May 1917: 'We find we have only 50 friends in the world – and most of them stingy. Could you think of any generous people – they need not be very generous – whose names you would send me?'

The advertisement, an amateur endeavour, in which even the price is wrong (the pamphlet was actually sold for 1s 6d), nonetheless showed their ambition: the words 'Publication No. 1' also appeared prominently on the title page of *Two Stories*, as it was finally named. The two short stories were Leonard's 'Three Jews' and Virginia's 'The Mark on the Wall'.

*

Orders started to arrive, and Virginia was busy setting Leonard's story; 'I haven't produced mine yet,' she told her sister. 'It was a casual mark of the utmost significance,' observes Virginia's biographer, Hermione Lee:

> For Leonard, the story was a signpost pointing down a road he would not take as a fiction writer, as a Jewish writer. But for Virginia it 'marked', as her title suggests, a completely new direction, the beginning of a new form and a new kind of writing.

The language of the title page was also unusual, being 'written and printed by Virginia Woolf and L.S. Woolf'. The composition of sentences, via the creative flow of fiction and their setting in individual Foundry letters, were inextricably linked. As Lee remarks, 'the new machine had created the possibility for the new story'.

By July, the texts were finally printed. Dora Carrington travelled to Hogarth House to deliver four commissioned woodcuts in person. Virginia thanked her: 'Will you let us know what your expenses (including fare, and one halfpenny newspaper) come to, so that your pittance may be doled out to you.' The Woolfs had tremendous difficulties printing the woodcuts – the blocks were too high and left smudged surrounds – but the images lent a lively, bold Omega style to the pamphlet.

The red and white Japanese paper covers were similarly arresting. The thread for binding, also a vivid red, was stab-stitched and knotted by Virginia. The red knot continues to be a powerful draw for those seeking a physical connection with her.

The print run of 134 copies (which nonetheless required over 4000 pulls on the printer on Leonard's part) sold out quickly, even when they raised the price of the last few copies to 2s. Receipts came to £10 8s with a net profit of £7 1s once costs of paper and ink and Carrington's fee of 15s were deducted. Leonard in particular took great pride and delight in the healthy figures. Almost immediately the Woolfs were looking for a larger printing machine, and an apprentice.

If fiction was not to be Leonard's ultimate direction, seven years as an administrator in Ceylon had taught him much about office management and meticulous accounting. His networks in politics and journalism, his honed commissioning instincts and excellent business sense, enabled him to steer a profitable course for the Press.

Virginia was inspired by her readers' reactions. 'I'm very glad you liked the story,' she replied to David Garnett:

> In a way its easier to do a short thing, all in one
> flight than a novel. Novels are frightfully clumsy
> and overpowering of course; still if one could only
> get hold of them it would be superb. I daresay one
> ought to invent a completely new form.

She had made her 'mark' – with a new and distinctive voice – and her story augured a change in her writing. It was 'very amusing to try with these short things,' she continued 'and the greatest mercy to be able to do what one likes – no editors, or publishers, and only people to read who more or less like that sort of thing.'

This was said through gritted teeth, as she would deliver her next novel, *Night and Day*, to the publishers Duckworth.

But at Hogarth House, with its green-carpeted dining room, she would also write the stories of *Monday or Tuesday*, the novel *Jacob's Room*, and embark on *Mrs Dalloway*. It was important that she and Leonard published these titles themselves, albeit now using out-of-house printers for longer books with substantial print runs. Not only did they expand the list to include many writers which, according to Leonard, 'the commercial publisher would not look at,' they also made room for their in-house writer Virginia. They had created a 'strange offspring', but it was a Press they could call their own.

CLARA FARMER
Publishing Director
Chatto & Windus and Hogarth

London, April 2017

FURTHER READING

For first-hand accounts, see Leonard Woolf's autobiographies, *Beginning Again* (1964) and *Downhill All The Way* (1967) and Virginia Woolf's *Diaries* (ed. Anne Olivier Bell and Andrew McNeillie, 1977–84) and *Letters* (ed. Nigel Nicolson and Joanne Trautmann, 1975–80). For a full-length work on the press, see J.H. Willis Jr, *Leonard and Virginia Woolf as Publishers: the Hogarth Press 1917–1941* (1992); a bibliography of early publications is provided by J. Howard Woolmer, *A Checklist of the Hogarth Press 1917–1946* (1986). For a biographical account, brilliantly contextualizing the Press in the life and work of the Woolfs, see Hermione Lee, *Virginia Woolf* (1996). For illustrations of the books themselves, see Elizabeth Willson Gordon's beautifully produced *Woolf's-head Publishing: the Highlights and New Lights of the Hogarth Press* (2009).

A NOTE ON THE TEXT

Two Stories does not appear to have gone through rigorous proofreading; or perhaps the Woolfs deemed the occasional misprint unimportant, once weighed against the job of dismantling the inked type and reworking the 'chase' to make a correction.

The text printed here, in a version of the Caslon font they used, follows the 1917 version of 'The Mark on the Wall', retaining words and phrases removed from later editions. But this is not intended as a facsimile, and any typos or missed spacings in the original have not been reproduced.

THE MARK ON
THE WALL

WRITTEN BY

VIRGINIA WOOLF

ILLUSTRATED BY

DORA CARRINGTON

THE MARK ON THE WALL

Perhaps it was the middle of January in the present year that I first looked up and saw the mark on the wall. In order to fix a date it is necessary to remember what one saw. So now I think of the fire; the steady film of yellow light upon the page of my book; the three chrysanthemums in the round glass bowl on the mantelpiece. Yes, it must have been the winter time, and we had just finished our tea, for I remember that I was smoking a cigarette when I looked up and saw the mark on the wall for the first time. I looked up through the smoke of my cigarette and my eye lodged for a moment upon the burning coals, and that old fancy of the crimson flag flapping from the castle tower came into my mind, and I thought of the cavalcade of red knights riding up the side of the black rock. Rather to my relief the sight of the mark interrupted the fancy, for it is an old fancy, an automatic fancy, made as a child perhaps. The mark was a small round mark, black upon the white wall, about six or seven inches above the mantelpiece.

How readily our thoughts swarm upon a new object, lifting it a little way, as ants carry a blade of straw so feverishly, and then leave it. . . . If that mark was made by a nail, it can't have been for a picture, it must have been for a miniature—the miniature of a lady with white powdered curls, powder-dusted cheeks, and lips like red carnations. A fraud of course, for the people who had this house before us would have chosen pictures in that way—an old picture for an old room. That is the sort of people they were—very interesting people, and I think of them so often, in such queer places, because one will never see them again, never know what happened next. She wore a flannel dog collar round her throat, and he drew posters for an oatmeal company, and they wanted to leave this house because they wanted to change their style of furniture, so he said, and he was in process of saying that in his opinion art should have ideas behind it when we were torn asunder, as one is torn from the old lady about to pour out tea and the young man about to hit the tennis ball in the back garden of the suburban villa as one rushes past in the train.

But as for that mark, I'm not sure about it; I don't believe it was made by a nail after all; it's too big, too round, for that. I might get up, but if I got up and looked at it, ten to one I shouldn't be able to say for certain; because once a thing's done, no one ever knows how it happened. O dear me, the mystery of life! The inaccuracy of thought! The ignorance of humanity! To show how very little control of our possessions we have—what an accidental affair this living is after all our civilisation—let me just count over a few of the things lost in our lifetime, beginning, for that seems always the most mysterious of losses— what cat would gnaw, what rat would nibble—three pale blue canisters of book-binding tools? Then there were the bird cages, the iron hoops, the steel skates, the Queen Anne coal-scuttle, the bagatelle board, the hand organ—all gone, and jewels too. Opals and emeralds, they lie about the roots of turnips. What a scraping paring affair it is to be sure! The wonder is that I've any clothes on my back, that I sit surrounded by solid furniture at this moment. Why, if one wants to compare life to anything, one must liken it to being blown through the Tube at fifty miles an hour— landing at the other end without a single hair pin in one's hair! Shot out at the feet of God entirely naked! Tumbling head over heels in the asphodel meadows like brown paper parcels pitched down a shoot in the post office! With one's hair flying back like the tail of a race horse. Yes, that seems to express the rapidity of life, the perpetual waste and repair; all so casual, all so haphazard. . . .

But after life. The slow pulling down of thick green stalks so that the cup of the flower, as it turns over, deluges one with purple and red light. Why, after all, should one not be born there as one is born here, helpless, speechless, unable to focus one's eyesight, groping at the roots of the grass, at the toes of the Giants? As for saying which are trees, and which are men and women, or whether there are such things, that one won't be in a condition to do for fifty years or so. There will be nothing but spaces of light and dark, intersected by thick stalks, and rather higher up perhaps, rose-shaped blots of an indistinct colour— dim pinks and blues—which will, as time goes on, become more definite, become—I don't know what.

And yet the mark on the wall is not a hole at all. It may even be caused by some round black substance, such as a small rose leaf, left over from the summer, and I, not being a very vigilant house-keeper—look at the dust on the mantelpiece, for example, the dust which, so they say, buried Troy three times over, only fragments of pots utterly refusing annihilation, as one can believe. But I know a house-keeper, a woman with the profile of a police-man, those little round buttons marked even upon the edge of her shadow, a woman with a broom in her hand, a thumb on picture frames, an eye under beds and she talks always of art. She is coming nearer and nearer; and now, pointing to certain spots of yellow rust on the fender, she becomes so menacing that to oust her, I shall have to end her by taking action: I shall have to get up and see for myself what that mark—

But no. I refuse to be beaten. I will not move. I will not recognise her. See, she fades already. I am very nearly rid of her and her insinuations, which I can hear quite distinctly. Yet she has about her the pathos of all people who wish to compromise. And why should I resent the fact that she has a few books in her house, a picture or two? But what I really resent is that she resents me—life being an affair of attack and defence after all. Another time I will have it out with her, not now. She must go now. The tree outside the window taps very gently on the pane. I want to think quietly, calmly, spaciously, never to be interrupted, never to have to rise from my chair, to slip easily from one thing to another, without any sense of hostility, or obstacle. I want to sink deeper and deeper, away from the surface, with its hard separate facts. To steady myself, let me catch hold of the first idea that passes. Shakespeare. Well, he will do as well as another. A man who sat himself solidly in an arm-chair, and looked into the fire, so—. A shower of ideas fell perpetually from some very high Heaven down through his mind. He leant his forehead on his hand, and people, looking in through the open door, for this scene is supposed to take place on a summer's evening,——But how dull this is, this historical fiction! It doesn't interest me at all. I wish I could hit upon a pleasant track of thought, a track indirectly reflecting credit upon myself, for those are the pleasantest thoughts, and very frequent even in the minds of modest mouse-coloured people, who believe genuinely that they dislike to hear their own praises. They are not thoughts directly praising oneself; that is the beauty of them; they are thoughts like this.

And then I came into the room. They were discussing botany. I said how I'd seen a flower growing on a dust heap on the site of an old house in Kingsway. The seed, I said, must have been sown in the reign of Charles the First. What flowers grew in the reign of Charles the First? I asked——(but I don't remember the answer). Tall flowers with purple tassels to them perhaps. And so it goes on. All the time I'm dressing up the figure of myself in my own mind, lovingly, stealthily, not openly adoring it, for if I did that, I should catch myself out, and stretch my hand at once for a book in self-protection. Indeed, it is curious how instinctively one protects the image of oneself from idolatry or any other handling that could make it ridiculous, or too unlike the original to be believed in any longer. Or is it not so very curious after all? It is a matter of great importance. Suppose the looking glass smashes, the image disappears, and the romantic figure with the green of forest depths all about it is there no longer, but only that shell of a person which is seen by other people—what an airless, shallow, bald, prominent world it becomes! A world not to be lived in. As we face each other in omnibuses and underground railways we are looking into the

mirror; that accounts for the expression in our vague
and almost glassy eyes. And the novelists in future
will realise more and more the importance of these
reflections, for of course there is not one reflection
but an almost infinite number; those are the depths
they will explore, those the phantoms they will pursue,
leaving the description of reality more and more out
of their stories, taking a knowledge of it for granted,
as the Greeks did and Shakespeare perhaps; but these
generalisations are very worthless. The military sound
of the word is enough. It recalls leading articles, cabinet
ministers—a whole class of things indeed which as a
child one thought the thing itself, the standard thing,
the real thing, from which one could not depart save
at the risk of nameless damnation. Generalisations
bring back somehow Sunday in London, Sunday
afternoon walks, Sunday luncheons, and also ways

of speaking of the dead, clothes, and habits—like the habit of sitting all together in one room until a certain hour, although nobody liked it. There was a rule for everything. The rule for tablecloths at that particular period was that they should be made of tapestry with little yellow compartments marked upon them, such as you may see in photographs of the carpets in the corridors of the royal palaces. Tablecloths of a different kind were not real tablecloths. How shocking and yet how wonderful it was to discover that these real things, Sunday luncheons, Sunday walks, country houses, and tablecloths were not entirely real, were indeed half phantoms, and the damnation which visited the disbeliever in them was only a sense of illegitimate freedom. What now takes the place of those things, I wonder, those real standard things? Men perhaps, should you be a woman; the masculine point of view which governs our lives, which sets the standard, which establishes Whitaker's Table of Precedency, which has become, I suppose, since the war half a phantom to many men and women, which soon one may hope will be laughed into the dustbin where the phantoms go, the mahogany sideboards and the Landseer prints, Gods and Devils, Hell and so forth, leaving us all with an intoxicating sense of illegitimate freedom—if freedom exists.

In certain lights, that mark on the wall seems actually to project from the wall. Nor is it entirely circular. I cannot be sure, but it seems to cast a perceptible shadow, suggesting that if I ran my finger down that strip of the wall it would at a certain point mount and descend a small tumulus, a smooth tumulus like those barrows on the South Downs which are, they say, either tombs or camps. Of the two I should prefer them to be tombs, desiring melancholy like most English people, and finding it natural at the end of a walk to think of the bones stretched beneath the turf. There must be some book about it. Some antiquary must have dug up those bones and given them a name. What sort of a man is an antiquary, I wonder? Retired colonels for the most part, I daresay, leading parties of aged labourers to the top here, examining clods of earth and stone, and getting into correspondence with the neighbouring clergy, which being opened at breakfast time gives them a feeling of importance, and the comparison of arrowheads necessitates cross-country journeys to the country towns, an agreeable necessity both to them and to their elderly wives, who wish to make plum jam or to clean out the study, and have every reason for keeping that great question of the camp or the tomb in perpetual suspension, while the Colonel himself feels agreeably philosophic in accumulating evidence on both sides of the question. It is true that he does finally incline to believe in the camp; and, being opposed, casts all his arrowheads into one scale, and being still further opposed, indites a pamphlet which he is about to read at the quarterly meeting of the local society when a stroke lays him low, and his last conscious thoughts are not of wife or child, but of the camp and that arrowhead there, which is now in the case at the local museum, together with the foot of a Chinese murderess, a handful of Elizabethan nails, a great many Tudor clay pipes, a piece of Roman pottery, and the wine-glass that Nelson drank out of— proving I really don't know what.

No, no, nothing is proved, nothing is known. And if I were to get up at this very moment and ascertain that the mark on the wall is really—what shall we say?——the head of a gigantic old nail, driven in two hundred years ago, which has now, owing to the patient attrition of many generations of housemaids, revealed its head above the coat of paint, and is taking its first view of modern life in the sight of a white-walled fire-lit room, what should I gain? Knowledge? Matter for further speculation? I can think sitting still as well as standing up. And what is knowledge? What are our learned men save the descendants of witches and hermits who crouched in caves and in woods brewing herbs, interrogating shrew-mice, and writing down the language of the stars? And the less we honour them as our superstitions dwindle and our respect for beauty and health of mind increases. . . . Yes, one could imagine a very pleasant world. A quiet spacious world, with the flowers so red and blue in the open fields. A world without professors or specialists or housekeepers with the profiles of policemen, a world which one could slice with one's thought as a fish slices the water with his fin, grazing the stems of the water-lilies, hanging suspended over nests of white sea eggs. . . . How peaceful it is down here, rooted in the centre of the world and gazing up through the gray waters, with their sudden gleams of light, and their reflections—if it were not for Whitaker's Almanack—if it were not for the Table of Precedency!

I must jump up and see for myself what that mark on the wall really is—a nail, a rose-leaf, a crack in the wood?

Here is Nature once more at her old game of self-preservation. This train of thought, she perceives, is threatening mere waste of energy, even some collision with reality, for who will ever be able to lift a finger against Whitaker's Table of Precedency?

The Archbishop of Canterbury is followed by the Lord High Chancellor; the Lord High Chancellor is followed by the Archbishop of York. Everybody follows somebody, such is the philosophy of Whitaker; and the great thing is to know who follows whom. Whitaker knows, and let that, so Nature counsels, comfort you, instead of enraging you; and if you can't be comforted, if you must shatter this hour of peace, think of the mark on the wall.

I understand Nature's game—her prompting to take action as a way of ending any thought that threatens to excite or to pain. Hence, I suppose, comes our slight contempt for men of action, men, we assume, who don't think. Still, there's no harm in putting a full stop to one's disagreeable thoughts by looking at a mark on the wall.

Indeed, now that I have fixed my eyes upon

it, I feel that I have grasped a plank in the sea; I feel a satisfying sense of reality which at once turns the two Archbishops and the Lord High Chancellor to the shadows of shades. Here is something definite, something real. Thus, waking from a midnight dream of horror, one hastily turns on the light and lies quiescent, worshipping the chest of drawers, worshipping solidity, worshipping reality, worshipping the impersonal world which is proof of some existence other than ours. That is what one wants to be sure of. . . . Wood is a pleasant thing to think about. It comes from a tree; and trees grow, and we don't know how they grow. For years and years they grow, without paying any attention to us, in meadows, in forests, and by the side of rivers—all things one likes to think about. The cows swish their tails beneath them on hot afternoons; they paint rivers so green that when a moor-hen dives

one expects to see its feathers all green when it comes
up again. I like to think of the fish balanced against the
stream like flags blown out; and of water-beetles slowly
raising domes of mud upon the bed of the river. I like
to think of the tree itself: first the close dry sensation
of being wood; then there is the grinding of the storm;
then the slow, delicious ooze of sap. I like to think of it
too on winter's nights standing in the empty field with
all leaves close-furled, nothing tender exposed to the
iron bullets of the moon, a naked mast upon an earth
that goes tumbling, tumbling, all night long. The song
of birds must sound very loud and strange in June;
and how cold the feet of insects must feel upon it, as
they make laborious progresses up the creases of the
bark, or sun themselves upon the thin green awning
of the leaves, and look straight in front of them with
diamond-cut red eyes. One by one the fibres snap

beneath the immense cold pressure of the earth; then the last storm comes and, falling, the highest branches drive deep into the ground again. Even so, life isn't done with; there are a million patient, watchful lives still for a tree, all over the world, in bed-rooms, in ships, on the pavement, lining rooms where men and women sit after tea smoking their cigarettes. It is full of peaceful thoughts, happy thoughts, this tree. I should like to take each one separately—but something is getting in the way. . . . Where was I? What has it all been about? A tree? A river? The Downs? Whitaker's Almanack? The fields of asphodel? I can't remember a thing. Everything's moving, falling, slipping, vanishing. . . . There is a vast upheaval of matter. Someone is standing over me and saying—

'I'm going out to buy a newspaper.'

'Yes?'

'Though it's no good buying newspapers. . . .
Nothing ever happens. Curse this war! God damn this
war! . . . All the same, I don't see why we should have
a snail on our wall.'

Ah, the mark on the wall! For it was a snail.